Too Sick To Sing

An Ivy and M

Contents

Written by Juliet Clare Bell

Illustrated by Gustavo Mazali

with Martyn Cain

Collins

What's in this story?

Listen and say

Download the audio at www.collins.co.uk/839734

singer

Chapter 1 The school concert

Ivy's teacher, Ms May, told the class about the school **concert**.

"I know you all love music and singing!" said Ms May. "Who would like to play in the orchestra?"

SCHOOL CONCERT

All the children in the class talked about the concert. Everyone wanted to do something.

Maddy put up her hand. "I can play the violin!" she said.

James put up his hand. "I can play the trumpet!" he said.

"Great," said Ms May. "We need singers, too. Who wants to sing?"

Ivy looked at Mina. Mina said nothing.

"*Please* sing in the concert?" said Ivy. "We can **practise** the songs at my house?"

"OK ..." said Mina **slowly**. She put up her hand, too.

Ivy and Mina went to the music room at break time.

"Our singers!" said Ms May. "Here's our book of songs."

Ivy and Mina listened to all the songs. "You can choose one to sing," said Ms May.

"Can we sing one **together**, too?" asked Ivy.

"Yes, you can," said Ms May. "Why don't you sing *'Two is better'* at the end of the concert?"

Ivy and Mina learnt their songs. Ms May looked up from the piano. "That was great!" she said.

Chapter 2 Time to practise

On Monday, Ivy practised with Mina in her bedroom.

Mack came in and Mina stopped singing.

"Can I listen to you?" asked Mack.

But Mina didn't want to sing to him.
"Sorry, Mack," said Mina.

Ivy practised her songs all week — in bed, in the bath, at dinner. And on Friday, she sang to Mack in his room.

But when Mina and Ivy practised at the weekend, Ivy closed the bedroom door.

The night before the concert, Mina came to Ivy's house for their **last practice** together. This time, she didn't close the door.

Ivy and Mina sang and Mack listened. It was beautiful.

Ivy went to the kitchen to get a drink of water. Mack was in the kitchen with Mum and Dad.

"Mina's singing is fantastic!" said Mack. "I *love* it!"

Ivy was sad. "Mack likes *Mina's* singing," she thought. "But he doesn't like *mine*!"

Chapter 3 I can't sing

That night, Ivy dreamt about the concert. Her singing was terrible and she made lots of mistakes.

Everyone loved Mina but they laughed at Ivy. Ivy woke up and cried.

Ivy cried and cried. She couldn't talk.

Mum came in. "**What's the matter**?" she asked.

Ivy had a very sad face. "I'm too sick to sing," she said **quietly**.

At school, Ivy talked to Mina.

"I'm sick. I can't sing," said Ivy.

"Oh no!" said Mina. "You need to sing your song. And you need to sing *'Two is better'* with me."

Ivy didn't look at Mina. "I can't. I'm too sick to sing. Can you sing your songs *and* my song?"

Mina looked sad. "But I like singing *'Two is better'* with you!"

"*Please?*" said Ivy.

Chapter 4 I can do it

In the evening, Ivy went to school to watch the concert. First, the school orchestra played some music.

Mack held her hand. "I'm sorry you're too sick to sing, Ivy."

"Thank you," said Ivy.

"And I'm sad," said Mack. Ivy looked at him.
"Why are *you* sad?"

"I wanted to watch you sing," said Mack.
"I love your singing!"

Ivy didn't understand. "But you like *Mina's* singing. You don't like my singing."

"Mina's singing is beautiful," said Mack. "But your singing is beautiful, too!"

"Is it?" asked Ivy.

Ivy stood up. She **hugged** Mack. "Mum! Dad! I'm not sick now," said Ivy and she ran to find Mina.

Ivy found Mina. "Are you **better** now?" asked Mina.

"Yes, I am. I want to sing!" said Ivy.

24

"I'm so happy," said Mina. "Now you can sing your song and we can sing *'Two is better'* together!"

Ivy smiled. "Yes, we can!"

Chapter 5 Well done!

Ms May started to play the piano.

"That's the music for the songs," said Mina. "Let's go!"

26

Mina sang her song and then Ivy sang hers.
Ivy's singing was strong and loud.

It was the end of the concert and time for the last song.

Ivy and Mina sang, *'Two is better'*.

Ivy looked at all the happy faces and saw Mack. Everyone clapped, but Mack clapped the loudest.

Mini-dictionary

Listen and read

better (adjective) Someone who is **better** is no longer ill.

concert (noun) A **concert** is a show when some people play music or sing for other people.

hug (verb) If you **hug** someone, you put your arms around them and hold them.

last (adjective) Something that is **last** is the only one that is left.

practice (noun) **Practice** is time you spend doing something so that you can do it better.

practise (verb) If you **practise** something, you do it a lot so that you can do it better.

quietly (adverb) If you speak **quietly**, you do not speak in a very loud voice.

slowly (adverb) If you speak **slowly**, you do not speak very quickly.

together (adverb) If people do something **together**, they do it with each other.

What's the matter? (phrase) If you ask **What's the matter?**, you want to know what is wrong.

1 Look and order the story

2 Listen and say

Collins

Published by Collins
An imprint of HarperCollins*Publishers*
Westerhill Road
Bishopbriggs
Glasgow
G64 2QT

HarperCollins*Publishers*
1st Floor, Watermarque Building
Ringsend Road
Dublin 4
Ireland

William Collins' dream of knowledge for all began with the publication of his first book in 1819.

A self-educated mill worker, he not only enriched millions of lives, but also founded a flourishing publishing house. Today, staying true to this spirit, Collins books are packed with inspiration, innovation and practical expertise. They place you at the centre of a world of possibility and give you exactly what you need to explore it.

© HarperCollins*Publishers* Limited 2020

10 9 8 7 6 5 4 3 2

ISBN 978-0-00-839734-0

Collins® and COBUILD® are registered trademarks of HarperCollins*Publishers* Limited

www.collins.co.uk/elt

British Library Cataloguing in Publication Data

A catalogue record for this publication is available from the British Library.

Author: Juliet Clare Bell
Lead illustrator: Gustavo Mazali (Beehive)
Copy illustrator: Martyn Cain (Beehive)
Series editor: Rebecca Adlard
Commissioning editor: Zoë Clarke
Publishing manager: Lisa Todd
Product managers: Jennifer Hall and Caroline Green
In-house editor: Alma Puts Keren
Project manager: Emily Hooton
Editor: Deborah Friedland
Proofreaders: Natalie Murray and Michael Lamb
Cover designer: Kevin Robbins
Typesetter: 2Hoots Publishing Services Ltd
Audio produced by id audio, London
Reading guide author: Julie Penn
Production controller: Rachel Weaver
Printed and bound by: GPS Group, Slovenia

MIX
Paper from
responsible sources

FSC
www.fsc.org

FSC™ C007454

This book is produced from independently certified FSC™ paper to ensure responsible forest management.

For more information visit: **www.harpercollins.co.uk/green**

Download the audio for this book and a reading guide for parents and teachers at www.collins.co.uk/839734